P9-CQY-442

APR 1 0 2003

RAISE THE ROOF!

WITHDRAWN

by Anastasia Suen

illustrated by Elwood H. Smith

viking

VIKING
Published by the Penguin Group
Penguin Putnam Books for Young Readers,
345 Hudson Street, New York, New York 10014, U.S.A.
Penguin Books Ltd, 80 Strand, London WC2R 0RL, England
Penguin Books Australia Ltd, 250 Camberwell Road, Camberwell, Victoria, 3124, Australia
Penguin Books Canada Ltd, 10 Alcorn Avenue, Toronto, Ontario, Canada M4V 3B2
Penguin Books (N.Z.) Ltd, 182-190 Wairau Road, Auckland 10, New Zealand

Penguin Books Ltd, Registered Offices: Harmondsworth, Middlesex, England

First published in 2003 by Viking,
a division of Penguin Putnam Books for Young Readers.

1 3 5 7 9 10 8 6 4 2

Text copyright © Anastasia Suen, 2003
Illustrations copyright © Elwood H. Smith, 2003
All rights reserved

LIBRARY OF CONGRESS CATALOGING-IN-PUBLICATION DATA
Suen, Anastasia.
Raise the roof! / by Anastasia Suen ; illustrated by Elwood Smith.
p. cm.
Summary: A family helps build their new house.
ISBN 0-670-89282-3
[1. House construction—Fiction. 2. Building—Fiction. 3. Stories in rhyme.]
I. Smith, Elwood H., date- ill. II. Title.
PZ8.3.S9354 Rai 2003
[E]—dc21
2002007459

Manufactured in China
Set in Clarendon
Book design by Teresa Kietlinski

The illustrations for this book were created using India ink
on 90 pound Arches cold press watercolor paper,
then scanned and colored in Photoshop.

For Cliff, one more time
—A.S.

For my high school art teacher,
Nancy B. Feindt
—E.H.S.

Make a plan.

Count the feet.

Clear the land
on this street.

Put in pipes here and there.

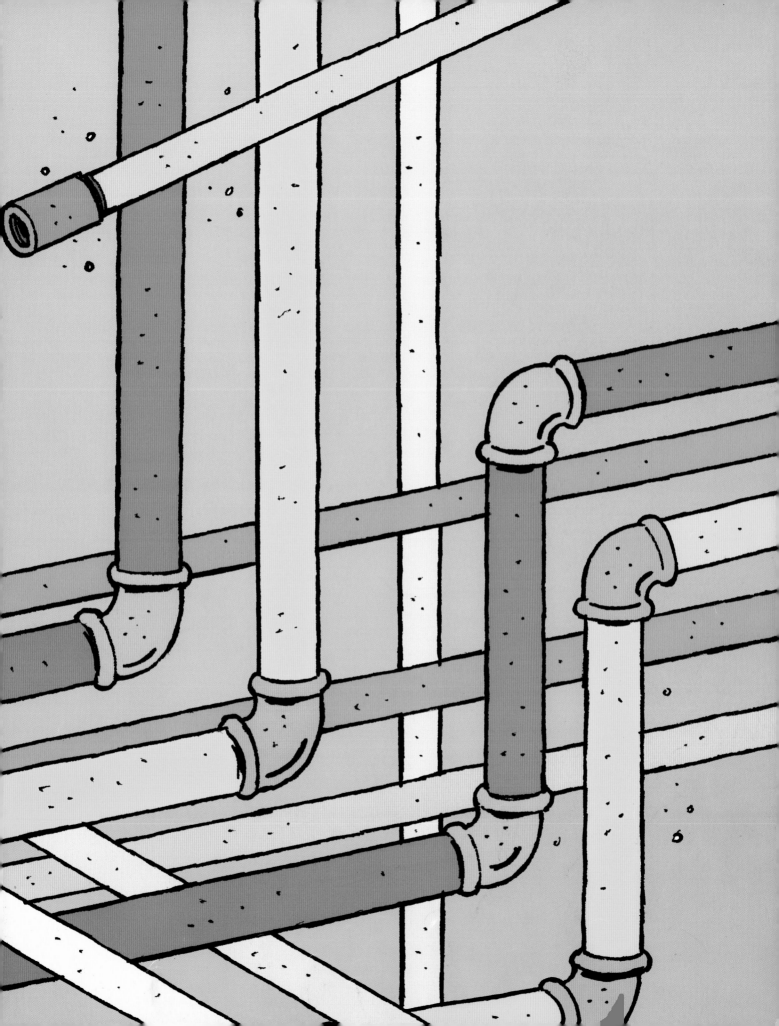

Pour concrete everywhere.

Saw the wood,
short and tall.

Hammer, hammer,
hammer it all.

Thread the wire
inside the walls.

Add more pipe.
Make it tall.

Put in windows

so you can see.

Cover the walls,
**one
two
three.**

Hang the doors,

big and small.

Now paint and paint

and paint it all.

Put in sinks.

Set the tile.

Roll out carpet
mile by mile.

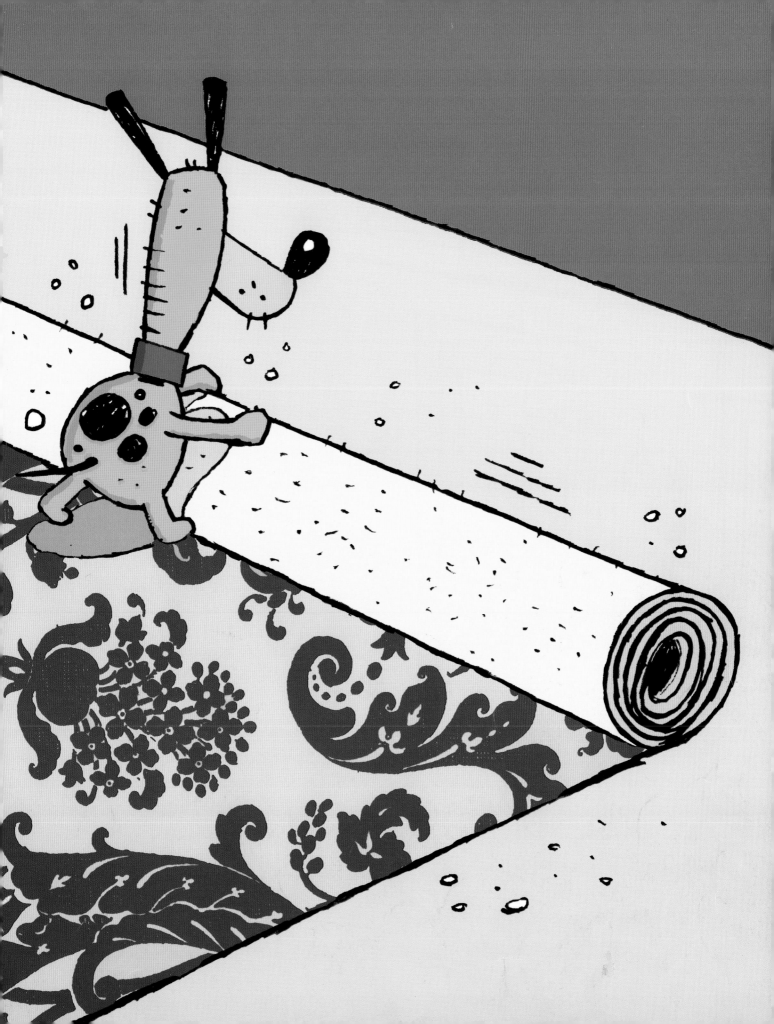

Plant the garden.
Water the grass.

The house is ready.

We're done

at last!